# The Boy and the Blue Balloon

## Kenneth Steven

Kenneth Steven, a young writer, is an active member of the Church of Scotland congregation in Aberfeldy, Scotland.

Illustrated by Lee Gallaher

Copyright © Kenneth Steven 1995

First published in 1995

Published by Autumn House
Alma Park, Grantham, NG31 9SL, England

ISBN 1-873796-44-7

There was a boy called Philip who lived in a house on the edge of a deep wood.

Early one morning he woke up and blinked at the sunlight coming through his window. Today was Monday, and he was on holiday from school. He was going exploring.

Philip crept downstairs, past his parents' room where his dad was snoring, and out into the back garden.

He reached the little gate at the edge of the wood and went through. Close by was a stream where he had found tadpoles.

This was beside the huge spreading boughs of the chestnut tree which scattered conkers on the grass every autumn. Philip loved the wood with its different trees and plants. He enjoyed feeding the birds that flew over into his garden, and looking out for the small animals like squirrels and hedgehogs.

He went towards his secret glade. This
was a clearing surrounded on all sides by
trees growing so close together it was a job to
squeeze between them. There Philip caught sight
of the top of something very strange. It was blue, and
looked as though it was hovering above the ground.

'What on earth can it be?' he thought to himself.
'No one is ever in this part of the wood but me. I must
find out.'

He pushed through the undergrowth, and there, to

his surprise, was a huge balloon with a basket fixed below it, gently swaying just above the ground.

Philip was excited. Without a sound he crept closer and closer over the soft grass. Then he reached out and touched it.

He had always dreamed of flying! Carefully he climbed in. He wanted to feel what it was like to stand in the basket. He bent down to look around inside when he felt the balloon move.

By the time he stood up he was already six feet in the air and climbing all the time. Philip had no time to be frightened, but he quickly whispered, 'Please God, be near me. Keep me safe.'

Now he and the balloon were as high as the tallest trees and as the balloon rose above them he could see his own house. He noticed that the curtains of his mum and dad's window were still tightly closed — what a shame they couldn't see him!

There was Simon's house down the lane, and further on Susan's. Now he was flying away from the village, going north, and climbing higher and higher.

'When will the balloon ever stop?' Philip thought, feeling the tiniest bit frightened now.

He didn't recognize the land he was flying over. The high hills seemed to rise up to meet him. He crossed a lake with many wild swans looking like little white dots. There were small islands in the lake.

On and on he went. He couldn't take in all there was to see.

Philip leant on the edge of the basket and watched the countryside going by below him, his mouth wide open with wonder at its beauty.

He had travelled such a distance he was feeling rather hungry and tired.

Now he was surprised to see that there was snow everywhere. He could hardly believe his eyes, because it had been summer at home when he left! He put his hands in his pockets to keep warm. As he looked down he saw deer trekking across the frozen ground. He was sure there must be wolves down there too!

Then ahead of him was nothing but a huge white emptiness. He gasped as he looked down and saw a tall tower made of blue-grey stone.

'It's like a dream I once had,' thought Philip. But this was no dream. Now the balloon was descending all by itself, circling like a bird around the tower until it landed gently on the snow.

Philip was now shivering with the cold.

'Welcome, my friend,' a kind voice called out.

Philip looked up and saw a very old man standing at the top of the stairs that wound around the tower. He wore a simple white robe and smiled at Philip. Then he beckoned him to come inside.

Philip ran up the stairs two at a time, glad to get

inside the tower out of the cold. There he gasped in amazement. On every side there were instruments and dials. On the benches were glass jars containing what looked like boiling liquid, and small round copper containers.

'I am the weatherman,' said the old man to Philip. 'I called you here for a very special reason. Come and look from this window.'

Philip looked out and saw many wonderful things, it was just like watching a film; clear waters and good land growing food, children running and playing, animals among the tall, golden woods.

But then a shadow fell over the scene and the children began to cry. The water was not pure any more but black with oil, and men were chopping down the trees.

'Make them stop!' Philip shouted, his eyes filling with tears at what he saw.

The weatherman bent close to him. 'I called you here, Philip, because *you* can help to make them stop.'

'Me?' Philip sniffed in surprise.

'Yes. God made all that beauty. He gave it to men and women, boys and girls, to look after. He looked at every thing and knew that He had made it perfectly. But men

were greedy. They wanted more and more for themselves, so they began stealing and fighting. Even when God sent Jesus they still wouldn't listen, even though He died for them.

'Now we have to tell others to be different, to follow Him and stop fighting, stop killing His beautiful world and making people hungry. Do you want that, Philip?'

Philip nodded.

'Yes, I will remember and do all I can to help,' he said.

'Then I am pleased I sent the balloon after all,' the weatherman said. He smiled happily as he turned to the food cupboard to prepare something warm for them both to eat.

CHIL

# Hide and Shriek!

## PAUL DOWLING

PUFFIN BOOKS

ALLSHARE

CHILLERS

**The Blob** Tessa Potter and Peter Cottrill
**Clive and the Missing Finger** Sarah Garland
**The Day Matt Sold Great-grandma** Eleanor Allen and Jane Cope
**The Dinner Lady** Tessa Potter and Karen Donnelly
**Ghost from the Sea** Eleanor Allen and Leanne Franson
**Hide and Shriek!** Paul Dowling
**Jimmy Woods and the Big Bad Wolf** Mick Gowar and Barry Wilkinson
**Madam Sizzers** Sarah Garland
**The Real Porky Philips** Mark Haddon
**Sarah Scarer** Sally Christie and Claudio Muñoz
**Spooked** Philip Wooderson and Jane Cope
**Wilf and the Black Hole** Hiawyn Oram and Dee Shulman

PUFFIN BOOKS

Published by the Penguin Group
Penguin Books Ltd, 27 Wrights Lane, London W8 5TZ, England
Penguin Books USA Inc., 375 Hudson Street, New York, New York 10014, USA
Penguin Books Australia Ltd, Ringwood, Victoria, Australia
Penguin Books Canada Ltd, 10 Alcorn Avenue, Toronto, Ontario, Canada M4V 3B2
Penguin Books (NZ) Ltd, 182–190 Wairau Road, Auckland 10, New Zealand

Penguin Books Ltd, Registered Offices: Harmondsworth, Middlesex, England

First published by A&C Black (Publishers) Ltd 1995
Published in Puffin Books 1996
3 5 7 9 10 8 6 4 2

Copyright © Paul Dowling, 1995
All rights reserved

The moral right of the author/illustrator has been asserted

Filmset in Meridien

Made and printed in England by William Clowes Ltd, Beccles and London

## Chapter One

HIDE AND SHRIEK!
A really scary story full of spiders, swirling mists, ghostly apparitions and jammy dodgers!

"Jammy dodgers! What's so scary about jammy dodgers?" you may be saying. Well…I know jammy dodgers are not something that you would normally associate with scary stories, but…

What if they looked like this –
and ate CHILDREN for breakfast?

Anyway, let's get on with the story,
because I'm...

# ...trembling to begin!

It's dark. Meg and Sophie are running at high speed along a gravel path.

"We'd better get off this noisy stuff!" said Sophie.

She jumped on to the grass and looked - back to see if he was following them.

In here!

Meg called as she dived deep into the middle of a big, leafy bush. She suspected there were bugs and worms and creepy, crawly things slithering about in there, but tried not to think about them. She knew it was more important to hide.

Sophie looked around. Meg was nowhere to be seen.

?

"Where?" she said.

"Inside this bush," said Meg.

Sophie crawled in.

Isn't this bush full of bugs and worms and creepy, crawly things?

Probably, but I was trying not to think about that!

The two friends peered cautiously out of
the bush. Everywhere was eerily quiet.
The trees were black against the purple
glow of the night sky. Suddenly, they saw
him. Creeping through the trees. The
dark, shadowy figure of **THE MAN!**

He stepped out from the trees and raised his arms to the sky. He threw back his head and cried out for all to hear:

YOU CAN'T HIDE FROM ME. NOBODY CAN HIDE FROM ME!

Then he laughed a ghastly, spooky, blood-curdling laugh. The sort of laugh that makes your hair stand on end, your eyes pop out, your jaw drop on to your chest, and sends the shivers running up and down your spine.

And that's exactly what it did to Meg and Sophie. Look I'll show you...

Meg and Sophie shook!

The bush shook!

The bugs shook!

The worms shook!

The creepy, crawly things shook!

Meg and Sophie gave each other
a big hug and said, "What are we
going to do?" They looked at each
other in the hope that the other had
some fantastic plan up HER sleeve.
But when they looked, all they
could find were small white
handkerchiefs,
which they
pulled out and
stuffed into their
mouths to stop
themselves squealing with fear.

"Fw fwaw fwa fweh," said Meg.

"Pardon?" said Sophie, after she'd pulled the handkerchief out of her mouth.

Meg pulled her handkerchief out of her mouth. "I said, we can't stay here."

And she was right, because if they did they would surely be caught, as easily as catching a bus.

Although, come to think of it, catching a bus isn't always that easy. I don't know about you, but I'm always missing buses.

I run out of my house and get to the bus-stop just as the bus is pulling away and have to stand there waiting for the next one, which is usually late or, worse still, has been cancelled altogether, and it's raining, and I haven't got an umbrella, and I get soaked, and the only thing I catch is a cold!

AAAACHOO!

BUS STOP

Bless you!

## Chapter Two

# The sh-sh-sh-shed!

The two girls scrambled out of the bush, ran through the long grass and hid in the shadows behind a large oak tree.

Oh no, Page 13!

Nearby was a small shed made of black corrugated iron. Stacked up against the walls were planks and lengths of wood. They stuck out above the roof like jagged fingers reaching out to touch the ivy that hung down from the overhanging branches of the oak tree. The door hung open on one broken hinge and the window was dirty and cracked.

"We could hide in there," said Sophie.

They looked at each other and gulped. Meg said:

Let's go and have a look.

The two girls stepped out of the shadows and immediately stopped dead in their tracks. They stared in horror at the window.

There, looking straight at them, were two ghostly pale faces. They were the scariest faces they had ever seen. Meg and Sophie gasped and jumped back behind the tree.

16

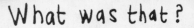

What was that?

That was the scariest thing I've ever seen, and that's the honest truth, scout's honour, cross my heart, swear on my great-great-granny's grave! The scariest thing I've ever seen!

Yeh, me too!

Now, I don't know about you, but at this point I would have said, "Come on, let's get out of here!" and run very fast in the opposite direction. And that is exactly what Sophie and Meg didn't do.

Maybe it was out of curiosity, or maybe it was because they were stark raving mad, but without saying a word they crept out from behind the tree and looked for a second time at the window of the shed.

The faces were
still there, and they
looked paler and scarier
than ever. But this time
Sophie stood and looked
straight at them, and after
a few moments she slowly
raised her arm and waved.
And do you know what?
One of the faces in
the window raised
its arm and waved
back. Then Meg
raised her arm and
waved, and the other
face in the window
raised its arm and waved back.

Then Sophie and Meg waved their other arms and the faces waved their other arms, and Sophie and Meg pulled faces and the faces pulled faces, and then

Meg giggled and said:

I knew it was our reflection straightaway.

And Sophie said:

Yes, so did I.

And they ran inside.

They should really have guessed that the doorway would be covered with cobwebs, but in all the excitement with the faces they didn't even think about it. So, the next thing that Meg said was:

"UUURRGH!"

And the next thing that Sophie said was:

"YeeeuuuRRGH!"

And there they were, covered from head to toe in sticky cobweb – trying to rub it off with their hands, and hoping that there hadn't been a spider sitting in the middle of the web. And trying not to think about where the spider might be now, if it *had* been sitting in the middle of the web, because it would probably be running through Sophie's hair or crawling over Meg's ear, looking for somewhere to hide.

And a really good place to hide would be down the neck of Sophie's shirt or up the leg of Meg's trousers.

Imagine it – a spider running up your trouser leg!

Meg and Sophie squirmed and wriggled and brushed frantically at their faces and clothes. And they would probably still be doing it now if a voice, right behind them, hadn't yelled:

AH-HA! NOW I'VE GOT YOU!

They turned around and there in the doorway stood *THE MAN!*

They were

TRAPPED!

He closed his eyes, leaped into the air and dropped to the hard ground below. He didn't hang around to see what would happen next, because the monsters were now dancing a weird dance, and were likely to stomp him into the ground at any moment. Look... here's a photograph taken by a reporter from **The Hairy Spider Gazette**, who just happened to be passing.

The spider scuttled into a crack in the wall and hid behind a broken brick, which was where his neighbour found him a few minutes later, and suggested a little walk back to her house for a sit down and a nice cup of tea, which is where he is now...
And he's looking a lot more cheerful than he did, isn't he?

# But wait! What about Meg and Sophie? We've left them trapped in the shed. With no escape except the door, which is blocked by *THE MAN!*

The two friends looked at each other.

*There's no choice!*

"CHARGE!" they shouted, and they bent their heads low and rushed headlong at the man.

Now, Meg and Sophie weren't very big but...

Their combined weight + high speed + the element of surprise (it was the last thing the man was expecting) = OI! WHAT'S GOING ON?

OOOF!

OUCH!

OI! COME BACK 'ERE!

CRASH!

Needless to say, Meg and Sophie didn't
wait around. They kept their heads down,
and ran and ran. And when they stopped
running, all they could hear was the
pounding of their own hearts. When they
looked back, all they could see was
darkness, and a swirling mist
that had billowed up
between the trees, and
they realised that they
had lost each other.

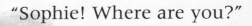

"Meg! Where are you?"
whispered Sophie.

There was no reply.

Some way away, Meg was searching about
in the mist.

"Sophie! Where are you?"

But there was
no reply.

They were lost.

# Alone.

**Just a Shaky Minute!**

I don't know about you, but I would not like to be in Meg's or Sophie's shoes right now.

Just think about it for a minute...

It's dark...

They're lost in swirling mist...

Someone is lurking in the darkness, just waiting for a chance to grab them...

Their best friend has disappeared...

And worst of all...they're all alone.

MY kn-knees are sh-sh-shaking!

## Chapter Three

# Does anyone know where I am?

Meg stood alone in the mist. She was cold and frightened. She tried to think.

"I mustn't panic," she told herself.

Which is easier said than done when you're in the sort of predicament that Meg was in! She decided that she should find somewhere safe to hide – somewhere she could take refuge – gather her thoughts – make a plan – suck her thumb!

She crept cautiously through the mist.

The first thing you notice when you're creeping cautiously through the mist is how difficult it is to see anything. In fact, all you can see is…mist! Then suddenly something looms up, just like that, right in front of you.

And that's exactly what happened to Meg.

One moment there was nothing and the next moment, there, right in front of her was…well, that was the trouble really, she didn't know what it was…

An eerie, dark shape, just hanging there in the mist.

Meg didn't know what it was! She cocked her head on one side, folded her arms and examined the strange, eerie shape in front of her. She would still be there if, from the swirling mist behind her, a horrible ghoulish voice, all too familiar to Meg, hadn't suddenly bellowed:

That was enough for Meg!
She no longer cared what it was hanging in the mist! She ran straight towards it.
She had to hide.

And luckily what was hanging there in the mist turned out to be...

| **B** | A BRICK WALL? | ✔ |

And the brick wall had a door in it, and as Meg crashed into it, it flew open. She tumbled through the doorway and found herself standing in a garage. She quietly closed the door and looked around.

Right in front of her was a car. The concrete floor underneath it was stained and dirty with oil. Beyond the car, in the wall opposite, were large double doors. In the wall to her right was a window. It was half obscured by a tall metal cupboard and curtained with some yellowish material. A plain, wooden table stood under the window with one end pushed up against the side of the cupboard.

On her left was an old chest of drawers with two bicycles and a scooter leaning on it. Three or four large sheets of thin plywood leaned against the wall, and in the far corner, stood a white freezer that buzzed and hummed continuously.

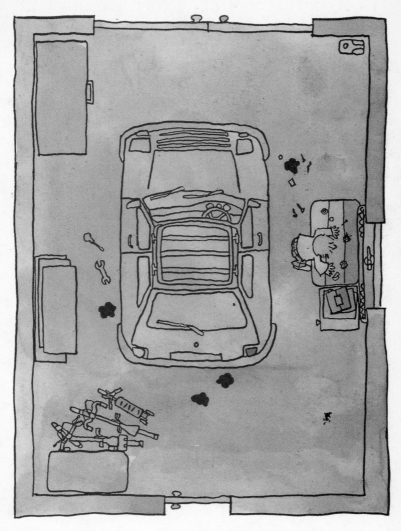

It was the only noise that Meg could hear
as she tiptoed over to the window, leaned
across the table, and peered out.

The sight that met her eyes filled her with horror.

There, emerging out of the mist, coming straight towards the garage, was **THE MAN!**

She ducked below the window and cast her eyes around, frantically searching for somewhere to hide.

She could hear heavy footsteps outside the garage door.

The door handle rattled.

Without thinking twice, Meg dived under the table, scrambled into the corner and sat with her back tight up against the wall. Then suddenly…

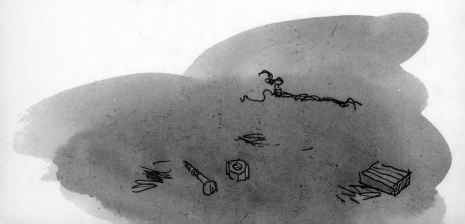

HOLD ON A MINUTE! Before I tell you
what happened next, I really ought to tell
you what had happened to Sophie when
she discovered she was **all alone.**

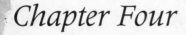

## Chapter Four

# What Sophie didn't manage to miss in the mist!

Sophie stood alone in the mist. She was cold and frightened. She looked around desperately but Meg was nowhere to be seen.

Then she saw a tree. At least she thought it was a tree. But the tree began to move. The branches first. They moved in the way branches move when there is a strong gust of wind. The trouble was, there was no wind! Then the trunk of the tree began to move and as it moved it turned its face towards Sophie and its eyes were deep dark shadows and it smiled a hideous smile....

Now, as you and I know perfectly well, trees have neither faces nor eyes, and as for trees smiling, well…it's completely ridiculous, and this is exactly what Sophie was thinking when the tree threw back its head, and shouted in a horrible ghoulish voice, that was all too familiar to Sophie:

YOU CAN'T HIDE FROM ME! NOBODY CAN HIDE FROM ME!

She ran.

But running through the mist in the dark is not easy. Things, as I have said before, suddenly appear. Things that weren't there suddenly are there.

And Sophie crashed into all of them.

She tripped over a  and stubbed her  .

**Yeowch!** she gasped under her breath. She bumped into a  and hurt her  just below the  .

**Oooch!** she cried under her breath. She ran too close to a  and scratched her  on the hanging  es.

**Yikes!** she wailed under her breath. And she fell over a

, did two forward and landed on her in a patch of stinging nettles.

**Oo, Owch, Ooo, Agh, OUCH!** she yelled, not under her breath, but quite loud in fact, because she'd had enough and was fed up, and wanted to be with Meg and didn't want to be in this swirling mist, being chased and bashing into things and hurting herself and falling into patches of stinging nettles.

39

Sophie felt like crying.

But at that moment, at that exact moment, something happened that made her forget all about crying. Something happened that made her blood freeze.

# SOMETHING TOUCHED HER BACK!

She sat absolutely still. She knew that if ever you found yourself face to face with a lion or a grizzly bear, you should stay absolutely still. She wondered if the same applied, when you were back to back with a lion or grizzly bear.

IT'S MY TURN!

The lion or grizzly bear or whatever it was, began to climb up her back. She felt its claws grip her shoulders. She felt its fur rub against her ear. She felt its warm breath on her neck. She felt its cold wet nose on her cheek.

# FACE to FACE

She turned her head, ever so slightly, hardly daring to look, and found herself with...

Meg's dog!

"Doug!" breathed Sophie, with not a little relief, "You really scared me!"

She gave Doug a big cuddle, and said, "Where's Meg, Doug?"

If Doug had been able to talk, he would have wagged his tail and said, "She's under the table in the garage, and she's scared because *he's* creeping around outside, and she wishes you were there!"

# Chapter Five

# Screwed, tacked, nailed, nutted and... *bolt!*

Meg was scared and wished that Sophie was there. She saw the door handle turning and the door slowly start to open.

For a moment, whoever was behind it was invisible. Then the door opened further and there, silhouetted in the open doorway, was *THE MAN!*

His head, swinging from left to right, hung forward like a vulture.

Meg hardly dared breath.

I know you're in there!

He stepped in, closed the door, stood quite still and listened. He walked over to the chest of drawers and pushed the bicycles to one side. He moved around the garage and searched behind the sheets of wood and down beside the freezer. He crossed the floor to the window, lifted the curtain and tried the catch. He walked over to the car, rubbed the windscreen with his hand and peered in. He went down on one knee and bent his head to check under the car. As he did, he turned, and looked towards the table.

Meg crouched back into the shadows and watched as his eyes narrowed to a hardly visible slit and he smiled a fiendish smile.

He'd seen her. This was it. She was cornered.

# T R A P P E D !

Now, at this point, it would not be unreasonable for you to assume that Meg is well and truly caught.

But wait…you're forgetting something. Meg has a best friend. And best friends are always there when their best friend needs a best friend most.

Sophie pushed the door hard. It opened wide and crashed against the inside of the garage wall.

The man's eyes flashed towards the door.

Meg leaped out from under the table.

The table rocked and knocked against the tall metal cupboard . . . bounced on the front edge of the cupboard . . . somersaulted through the air . . . and the box that was on which shook and wobbled . . . and the boxes piled on top swayed and teetered . . . the very top toppled off

And landed upside-down on
the man's head, spewing
out its contents…

Screws, tacks, nails, nuts and bolts showered down the man's coat and skidded across the concrete floor like insects. They went sliding under the car, rattling under the freezer, skimming under the table, bouncing off the walls and ricocheting into the dark corners behind the cupboards and boxes.

The man sat with his legs spread out in front of him, the cardboard box wedged firmly on his head. He lifted the flap that was hanging down in front of his face and watched Meg run out of the door.

## Chapter Six

# Creeping, seeking and shrieking!

He pulled the box off his head, stood up and walked around the car to the garage door. The mist was thicker than ever and there was no sign of the two girls. He listened.

A small nail slipped out of his hair. It fell on to his shoulder, rolled down the front of his coat and fell silently into the grass.

"They can't be very far," he muttered to himself. Then he heard…

They were running along the gravel path.

He raced across the grass taking long certain strides. They were off the path now. Two faint shadows, bounding up the steps and into the house.

He ducked down behind a bench as Meg and Sophie looked back from behind the half-closed door.

"We've lost him," whispered Sophie, "Switch off the light."

They closed the door.

And behind the bench, just a few metres away from the door, the man smiled, and whispered to himself:

He crept along beside the wall, and turned
the corner to the back of the house. The
door was locked. He checked the
windows. One was open. He hauled
himself up on to the window sill, swung
his legs over, and lowered himself silently
on to the carpeted floor. He closed the
window, turned, and looked around.

He was in a small bedroom. On his left
was a single bed, made up and covered
with a patterned bedcover that hung
down almost to the floor.

The wall above the bed was covered with posters and small pictures. A wardrobe stood against the right-hand wall. It had an old-fashioned brass handle on each of its two doors. One door was slightly open.

Further along the wall there was a glass-topped dressing table and mirror with a small upholstered stool tucked under it. A dark-coloured jumper lay loosely over the stool, the tips of its arms just brushing the carpet. In the centre of the end wall was a door. It was closed.

The room was still.

The only sound was the slow, dull tock of a small electric alarm clock. It was 8.59.

The man took a step forward.

The whole room shook and the man
gasped with terror as Meg shot out from
under the bed and grabbed his ankles.
At the same moment, Sophie leaped out
of the wardrobe, hurled a dressing gown
over his head and jumped on to his back.
Meg yanked at his legs. He lost his balance
and fell with a thump to the floor.
Sophie sat on his back as Meg
tied his arms together with
the thin orange cord from
the dressing gown. They
slipped a
trouser
belt under
his ankles,
pulled the loose
end over, threaded
it through the buckle
and pulled it tight.

# AAAARRGH!

The man groaned.

Meg and Sophie stood up
and looked at each other.

"Give me five," said Meg
and held out her hand.

Sophie grinned, raised her hand and
slapped it down on Meg's open palm.

"Let's go!" said Sophie and they stepped
over the moaning man, opened the door,
closed it and were gone.

57

*Chapter Seven*

# One lump or two?

And where do you think they went?

No, not to the nearest phone to call the police and report they had just caught a would-be murderer. And to tell them to get round here real quick and arrest him because they were frightened he might escape and suddenly appear at the door.

He'd be really angry because he'd been outwitted by two small girls. And murder them double quick, with no messing. And throw them in the back of his van, and drive to some deserted lay-by. And squash them into a litter bin. And leave their legs sticking out!

That'll teach 'em!

And go home and drink six pints of beer.

And shake his fist at his next door neighbour. And invent an alibi, so that if the police did come around, he could say:

I was down the pub!

or

...up the shop!

or

...fixing me car!

or

...on the loo!

And he'd get away with it and the police would cross him off their list of suspects, and stamp

across the front of the file, and put it in a drawer and forget about it. Until one day, years later, when the police station was having a spring clean, someone would find it and say, "What shall I do with this, Sarge?" and Sarge would say, "Oh, that old thing!" and throw it in the bin. And Meg and Sophie would be forgotten for ever and ever and…

# But wait a minute! What am I talking about?

Nobody's been murdered and Meg and Sophie didn't phone the police.

No...what they did, was this.

They walked into the kitchen, switched on the light, pulled out two stools and sat down.

Then Meg said, "That was fun."

And Sophie said, "Yeh. I was really scared."

And Meg said, "Yeh. So was I."

And a minute or two later, an extremely dishevelled, scruffy man shuffled into the kitchen, holding a leather belt and trailing an orange dressing gown cord which was tied around one wrist. He put the belt on the table, rubbed his head, smiled and said, "Anyone fancy a cup of tea and a jammy dodger?"

Meg looked at Sophie.

"Yes please," said Sophie.

"Yes please, Dad," said Meg.

And they sat there whilst Dad made a pot of tea, and they drank it, and they ate their jammy dodgers. They told each other what had happened to them.

And they laughed and giggled, and drank more tea and ate more jammy dodgers, and...oh yes...I suppose you're saying, "Where're the jammy dodgers with the eyes and the teeth that you told us about at the beginning of this story?"

Well...I have to tell you that, whereas the rest of this story is completely true, and I should know because I was there, there really is no such thing as a jammy dodger with eyes and teeth, that eats children for breakfast...is there?

No... but I do like a nice juicy writer for dinner!
Can I have this bit mum?
AAA-AAAA AAAG